Library of Congress Cataloging-in-Publication Data

Kroll, Steven.
Happy Father's Day.

SUMMARY: Each of the children and Mom have a special
surprise for Dad on his special day.
[1. Fathers—Fiction.   2. Family life—Fiction]
I. Hafner, Marylin, ill.   II. Title.
PZ7.K922Hao   1988   [E]   87-7559
ISBN 0-8234-0671-7

HAPPY FATHER'S DAY

by STEVEN KROLL

illustrated by MARYLIN HAFNER

HOLIDAY HOUSE   NEW YORK

For fathers everywhere

S. K.

For DOUGLAS, one of the best

M. H.

One morning, when Dad woke up, there was a note
on his lampshade.

Dad got washed and dressed. Then he hurried downstairs to the kitchen.
On the table was his favorite breakfast:

orange juice,

a roll,

and coffee.

a tall glass filled with
fresh fruit and yogurt,

Beside the coffee cup was a note:

TO START YOUR DAY
A SPECIAL WAY!
LOVE, LENNY
P.S. WHEN YOU'VE EATEN
BREAKFAST LOOK
BEHIND THE KITCHEN
DOOR.

"My goodness, I feel spoiled already," said Dad.
He sat down at the table and ate his breakfast.
"Delicious!" he said. Then he looked behind the
kitchen door.

"Surprise!" yelled Lenny, jumping out with a
Green Sox pennant. "I made this just for you."

"Thank you, Lenny," said Dad. "I'll hang it in my study."
"Now you have to come with me," said Lenny.

Lenny led Dad to a corner of the laundry room. The kitty litter had been changed. Taped to the side of the litter box was a note:

You hate to do it. Now it's done! Love, Linda

"Wow!" said Dad. "What a relief."

Linda sprang out from beside the washing machine. "Surprise!" she shouted. She held up a pair of green socks she had made.

"These are great," said Dad. "I'll wear them every time I play ball."

Dad followed Linda and Lenny out the back door.
All the garbage had been emptied and packed neatly
into plastic bags. On one of them was a note:

No Garbage For You on Father's Day! Love, Laurie

"You kids are too much," said Dad.

"Surprise!" shouted Laurie, crawling out from behind the garage with a Green Sox baseball cap in her hand.

Dad put on the baseball cap. "I've always wanted one of these," he said.

"Now you have to come with me," said Laurie. "There's another surprise."

Dad followed Laurie, Linda, and Lenny around the corner of the house.

The cellar door was freshly painted gray. Beside it was a sign:

"I meant to do that weeks ago," said Dad.

"Surprise!" shouted Louise, leaping out from behind a hedge. She was holding a Green Sox sweatshirt with *DAD* sewn on the back.

Dad put the sweatshirt on. "You're making me feel like a king," he said.

"You are a king!" said Lenny, Linda, Laurie, and Louise.

"But now you have to come with me," said Louise.

Dad followed Louise, Laurie, Linda, and Lenny
around to the front of the house.

The lawn was freshly mowed.

On the fence was a note:

"I'll buy that," said Dad.

"'Surprise!" shouted Larry, running out from behind the tree in the front yard. He held up a Green Sox key chain he had carved out of a block of wood.

Dad put the key chain in his pocket. "This family sure knows how to treat a Green Sox fan," he said.

Dad followed

Larry,

Louise,

Laurie,

Linda, and

Lenny

around to the terrace.

Baby Lester was sitting in his playpen.
On the side was a note:

Mom helped me
weed between the
flagstones. But I
did most of it.
Now you have to
come with me. There's
ANOTHER SURPRISE.
love, Lester

Larry picked up Lester, and Dad followed Lester, Larry, Louise, Laurie, Linda, and Lenny over to the garage.

Dad's car was sitting in the driveway. It had just been washed. It gleamed in the sunlight.

Taped to the windshield was a note:

"Surprise!" shouted Mom, jumping out from behind the wheel.

She held out tickets for the Green Sox game that afternoon.

"We're all going!" she said.

Dad hugged Mom. "What a wonderful day! Margaret, did you, was this—?"

"We planned it together," said Mom.

Dad smiled at everyone. "Well, let's get going!" he said.

Louise, Laurie, Linda, and Lenny piled into the back seat with baby Lester. Dad sat up front with Larry. Mom drove.

When they reached the stadium, Mom popped open the trunk of the car. "There's one more thing," she said.

"I can't believe there's more," said Dad.

Inside the trunk was a jumbo pizza. On the box was written:

HAPPY
FATHER'S DAY
TO THE
MOST TERRIFIC
DAD!

Dad beamed. "You guys are the greatest!" he said.

And Mom, baby Lester, Larry, Louise, Linda,
Laurie, and Lenny replied,

"YOU'RE THE GREATEST, DAD!"

Together they carried the pizza up to their seats.
And together they spent a wonderful afternoon
watching the game.